The Legend of LIZARD LICK

A North Carolina Folktale

Written by Karen Matthews

Illustrated by Josh Taylor

ISBN: 1479382477

ISBN 13: 9781479382477

Library of Congress Control Number: 2012917939

CreateSpace Independent Publishing Platform

North Charleston, South Carolina

The Legend of LIZARD LICK

Written by Karen Matthews
Illustrated by Josh Taylor

One day, little Carson went to visit his grandfather in the little community of Lizard Lick, North Carolina. He hopped up on his Grandpa's knee and asked, "Papa Richard, how did Lizard Lick get its name?"

"Well Carson, it's a very interesting story. It happened many years ago during the great drought at Sweetwater Pond."

"What is sweet water, Papa Richard?" asked Carson.

"Hmm," said Papa Richard. "Sweet water is the pure, crystal clear water that comes from the spring that feeds into Sweetwater Pond. It was so fresh and clean tasting that it was called sweet water."

Anyway, let me tell you how Lizard Lick got its name. It happened when Chuck Walla was Mayor of Lizard Town that was located at the edge of Sweetwater Pond. Mayor Walla's wife was named Ana Nole. She, and their son, Skinky, lived with him. Broadhead Billy was the Chief of Police of Lizard Town. He lived with his wife, Zora Zebra-tail, and their two children, Lickety Split and Snap Dragon.

Other members of the Lizard community were Turf Toe, his wife, Rock Dwella, and their son, Leapin' Larry. Turf Toe was one of Lizard Town's deputies and so was the handsome young lizard, Cricket Hunter.

Match the lizards with their pictures.

On the Balcony (left to right): Skinky, Ana Nole, Mayor Chuck Walla. Center, behind the town sign (left to right): Turf Toe, Leapin' Larry, Rock Dwella. Left, in front of the town sign: Zora Zebra-Tail, Broadhead Billy, Lickety Split, and Snap Dragon. Bottom right, Cricket Hunter.

In the middle of the pond, a community of frogs lived on a flotilla of lily pads. The mayor of Frogville was Hairy Frog. His wife was named Webfoot Wanda. They had two children, a daughter named Lila Pad and a baby son named Tiny Tad.

Bullfrogger was Frogville's Chief of Police. He lived with his wife, Hoppy Hazel, and their son, Tree Darter. Frogville's deputies were named Croaker and Flycatcher.

Toad Runner was the track and field coach at Frogville High. He was married to a frog language teacher named Frolicka. They had two children—a son named Dexter and a daughter named Swimmy.

Match the frogs with their pictures.

Top (left to right): Lila Pad, Tiny Tad, Webfoot Wanda, and Hairy Frog. In the window: Hoppy Hazel. Center (left to right) Croaker, Flycatcher, Chief Bullfrogger, and Tree Darter. Bottom (left to right) Swimmy, Frolicka, Dexter, and Coach Toad Runner.

Before the great drought, the lizards and frogs were friends. The lizards would greet the frogs when they'd meet at the pond's edge and say, "A lickin' lovely day to you."

The frogs would answer back, "A croakin' good day to you, too!"
They'd even celebrate holidays together—like Pondfest and Sweetwater
Days.

However, as the pond began to dry up during that terribly hot summer, every-thing changed. The water shrunk away from Lizard Town, and the lizards had to fetch their water in the muddy pond bed next to the lily pads.

   This bothered the frogs greatly. They began to complain to Mayor Hairy Frog that the lizards were occupying their space and disturbing their habitat. Mayor Frog asked Chief Bullfrogger to handle it.

The next day Rock Dwella and Ana Nole went near the lily pads to fetch some sweet water. When Chief Bullfrogger saw them, he told Croaker and Flycatcher to hurl pond fronds and twigs at the lady lizards.

Ana Nole gave Chief Bullfrogger a stern look and said, "What are you doing?"

The two lady lizards scurried back to Lizard Town. They headed straight to Mayor Chuck Walla to complain. Ana Nole was out of breath and told her husband, "One of those twigs missed my head by inches!"

"They are not going to get away with this," said Mayor Walla. "Sweetwater Pond is for all of us."

Chief Broadhead rounded up his deputies, Turf Toe and Cricket Hunter. When they got to the mud hole next to the lily pads, they started firing pebbles at the frogs' homes, one after another.

Webfoot Wanda looked at her husband, Hairy Frog, and said, "Mayor, what are you going to do, have an all out war with the lizards? We've lived in peace with them for all these years."

Coach Toad Runner piped up and said, "Let's propose a sports challenge. The winner of the tournament will get to stay in Sweetwater and the loser will have to leave."

"Great idea," said Swimmy, the coach's daughter. "I'm sure I could beat them in a swimming race."

The next day, Mayor Frog, Coach Toad Runner, and Chief Bullfrogger marched over to Lizard Town and knocked on the door of the town hall.

Cricket Hunter opened the door. "What do you want?" he said.

"We want to talk to Mayor Walla," they said.

Mayor Frog said to Mayor Walla, "We came to challenge you to a track and field tournament. The winner gets to stay in Sweetwater. The loser must leave."

"What type of sports contest?" asked Mayor Walla.

"The long jump, a ten-meter run, and a swimming race," said Coach Toad Runner.

"Ha, ha, ha." Mayor Walla laughed, "You know lizards can't swim. I'll tell you what—let the final event be a tug of war and we'll meet you at the hollow tree."

For the next few weeks, the lizards and frogs prepared their contestants for the big tournament.

After much practicing, the best of the frogs were chosen for each event. Croaker would be their long jumper, and Tree Darter would be their runner. Coach Toad Runner picked their six strongest frogs for their tug of war team.

The lizards had their try-outs and chose Leapin' Larry to represent them in the long jump. Lickety Split was the fastest runner and wore lucky number seven on his shirt.

The lizards were short on muscle and had to choose some of the youngsters like Skinky and Lickety Split for the tug-of-war team.

All the lizards chosen to represent Lizard Town trained very hard to get ready for the big contest, but they were a little worried about the weakness of their tug-of-war team.

The day of the big event arrived. Mayor Chuck Walla and Mayor Frog agreed ahead of time that Hoot Owl should be the referee. "We trust you will be fair," said Mayor Walla.

The frogs were hopping all around with excitement. The lizards stretched their muscles.

Mayor Walla and Mayor Frog shook hands to begin the games.

Leapin' Larry lined up even with the hollow tree. Hoot Owl gave the signal with a wave of his wing, and Leapin' Larry took a shot up in the air. Coach Toad Runner measured the jump. Four feet and three inches was the measurement.

Next, Croaker took his place by the hollow tree. He squatted really low and jumped up with all of his might. His jump measured five feet and one inch.

Hoot Owl proclaimed Croaker the winner. The frogs jumped for joy! The lizards were sad, especially Larry, who felt that he'd let his fellow lizards down.

Next, Tree Darter and Lickety Split lined up at the hollow tree for the foot race. Hoot Owl stood at the finish line at mossy stump. He raised his wing and said, "One, two, three, go!"

The frogs' best runner and the lizards' best runner were on their way.

The race was neck and neck, but in the final few seconds, Lickety Split jumped out ahead and crossed the finish line seconds before Tree Darter. Hoot Owl declared Lickety the winner.

After two contests, the score was even: Frogs 1, Lizards 1. The final event—the tug of war—would be the tiebreaker. It would decide who got to stay in Sweetwater Pond and who must leave.

Before they began, the lizards and frogs shouted bad words at each other and made ugly gestures.

The lizards lined up on the left and the frogs on the right. The six team members for each side grabbed a hold of the rope and held on tight.

The lizards started strong right off the bat—dragging the frogs close to the middle line. The lady lizards went wild with excitement.

Then Coach Toad Runner shouted, "Give it all you got, froggers!"

The frogs responded by tugging hard and started to move the lizards to the right–one foot, two feet...

Suddenly, Flycatcher stumbled. The lizards gained the advantage and with one big heave ho, the lizards dragged the frogs past the mid mark.

"Hurray! Hurray!" shouted the lizards. "We won!"
The frogs hung their heads in defeat.

"And that's how Lizard Lick got its name, Carson," said Papa Richard. "It was because the lizards licked the frogs in the track and field contest during the great drought at Sweetwater Pond."

"Papa Richard," said Carson. "Did the frogs have to leave the pond like they were supposed to? That's kind of sad."

"The story isn't over yet," said Papa Richard.

Mayor Frog said to Mayor Walla, "Well, Mayor Walla, you won fair and square. I guess we'll be packing up and finding another pond to live in."

Mayor Walla felt sorry for the frogs. After all they used to be friends. "I tell you what Mayor Frog—if you agree not to ever keep us from Sweetwater Pond again, we'll let you stay. That is, if the lizards agree. What do you say, lizards?"

"Sure yeah, let them stay," shouted the lizards.
At that moment, a big cloudburst poured rain all over their heads.

30

The lizards and frogs couldn't believe it and stuck out their tongues to lick the rain that was falling down all over them. Sweetwater Pond filled to overflowing. The great drought was finally over, and the lizards and frogs were friends again.

Note to Parents:

Lizard Lick is a tiny hamlet in North Carolina located about 22 miles northeast of Raleigh. Nobody knows for sure how the community really got its name, though there are some rumors floating about that have to do with moonshine, government stills, and lizards licking liquor on a fence. The author and illustrator prefer to tell this whimsical "made for children" version of the origins of Lizard Lick.

This book is a product of Carolina Souvenirs, a company that is developing unique souvenirs for the North Carolina and South Carolina tourist markets.

www.carolinasouvenirs.com